I0757480

Me and My Boo

Life with My Pacifier

Michelle Beetz

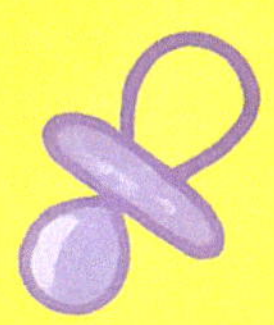

For my sweet Kendall,

From the moment you came into this world, you have filled our lives with sunshine, laughter, and love. At just three years old, you remind us every day that childhood is made of little joys—like cuddles, giggles, and treasures we hold close to our hearts.

This book is for you, my brave girl. Just like Boo, you show us that it's okay to find comfort in the things we love, and that growing up doesn't have to happen all at once. It happens in your own perfect time.

I hope whenever you open these pages, you remember how loved you are—not only today, but every single day of your life. May this story always remind you that courage, comfort, and love live inside your heart.

With all my love,
Grandma

My name is Kendall. I'm brave, bold, and super smart.
But I've got a secret... I still love my pacifier-my Boo.

Boo helps me when I feel shy.
When I'm sad or sleepy,
Boo is always nearby.

I bring Boo in the car, in my bed,
and sometimes even to the store.
Mama says Boo has been everywhere I go.

But lately, I've been wondering...
What if I don't need Boo as much as before?

Mama says when I'm ready,
we can find a special way to say goodbye.
Only when I'm ready.

We made a boo box just for me.
A place to keep Boo safe-when it's time.

I practice being brave,
just a little each day.
One nap. One story.
One night without Boo.

Sometimes, I miss Boo a lot.
That's okay. Feelings are big and real.

Other times, I feel like a superhero!
No Boo, just me-and I'm still okay.

One morning, I wake up and smile.
I didn't even think about Boo.

I open my Boo Box and whisper,
'Thank you for helping me grow.'

Mama and I do a little happy dance.
We celebrate the big steps I've taken.

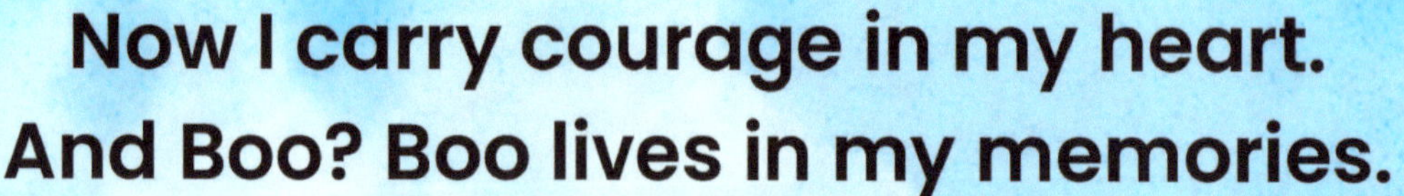

Now I carry courage in my heart.
And Boo? Boo lives in my memories.

I still have big feelings.
And I'm learning new ways to feel safe and strong.

Sometimes, brave looks like letting go.
Sometimes, brave looks like holding on.

I'll always remember my Boo.
And I'll always remember how brave I am.

And when another little one asks,
'Will I ever be okay without mine?'
I'll say, 'Yes, you will.'

Because brave kids grow big hearts
And mine just got a little bigger.

Goodbye Boo
CERTIFICATE

This certificate is proudly awarded to

____

for bravely saying goodbye to Boo,
their special pacifier.

Your brave heart shines bright!

Signed with love: ______________

Boo!

DRAW YOUR BOO
This is what my Boo looked like!

Also from Brooks Club

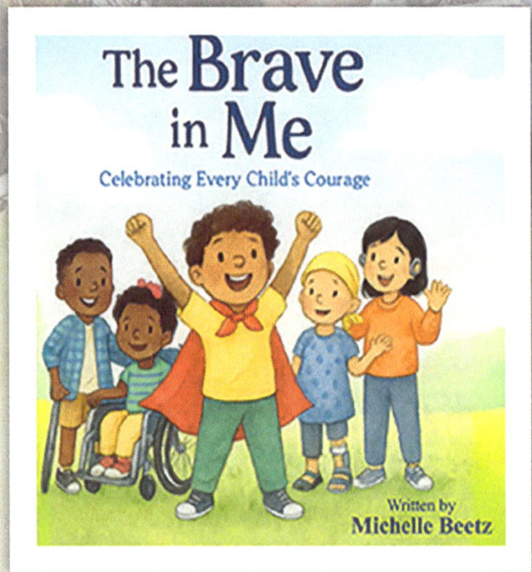

THE BRAVE IN ME

A heartwarming celebration
of everyday courage

BOO WHO?

A sweet Halloween tale about a
ghost who learns kindness

Upcoming Books

ME AND MY BOO

A tender story of letting go
and growing brave

JUST CHICKEN AND FRIES

Inspired by real kids with ARFID,
a story of self-acceptance and bravery

Stories that inspire courage, kindness, and hope for every child

www.brooksclubonline.com   Follow along: @brooksclubbooks